Shelly's Shell Search

Written by
Tracey Herrold

Illustrated by
Alexandra Lee

Just north of Moss Pond, down Lillypad Lane
lived a turtle named Shelly with a shell oh so plain.
This dusty green dome with a simple design
for the most part seemed to suit Shelly just fine.

For sunning or diving or splashing around
the shell was just perfect, Shelly had found.
It kept her skin safe from the sun's harshest glare
and it was waterproof too—the perfect sportswear!

Then one bright, sunny day a fancy note came.
In elegant script, it bore Shelly's name.
What could it be? Shelly thought as she tore
the envelope open so she could learn more.

"Dear creatures," it read, "Come one and come all
to the event of the season, the Dragonfly Ball.
The dancing will start at a quarter past nine
at the edge of the meadow beyond the lone pine."

As she read through the note, Shelly's turtle heart pounded.
A ball in the woods! She was truly astounded.
All she could think of was that special night
and the way she would twirl in the golden moonlight.

But then Shelly realized that for this gala affair
the fashion was festive—now what would she wear?
Her plain, dusty shell would simply not do;
for the Dragonfly Ball, she would need something new.

So she went into town where she knew of a place
that sold beautiful shells, perhaps one to replace
the plain old green one that had served her so well.
Yes, she wanted a bright one, a fancy new shell.

At Sheldon's Shell Shop, she saw an aquamarine one,
a most gorgeous shell, if ever she'd seen one.
It was exquisitely shaped, it curved like a horn,
a more elegant shell had never been worn.

She would ask the store clerk if she might try it,
and if it fit on her body, she thought she might buy it.
She imagined herself dancing in this fine, fancy shell.
She'd be the life of the party, the ball's beautiful belle.

But when she asked the clerk if she might give it a try,
the clerk shook her head snidely and said with a sigh,
"While you're right that this shell will make you less
drab, I'm afraid, madam, that it was made for a crab."

How embarrassing, Shelly thought with chagrin.
A hermit crab's shell, I'd never fit in.
I'll just have to keep looking for one not as tight.
I'll soon find a shell that will fit me just right.

So slowly she walked up, then slowly back down
the road that went through the middle of town.
And suddenly, right underneath Shelly's nose
was a sparkly red dome, the perfect new clothes.

So up Shelly slithered, into the sparkly red shell,
she wiggled and wriggled—it seemed to fit well.
Closing her eyes, thoughts swam through her head
of her night at the ball in a shell of bright red.

But then Shelly heard from beneath her new shell
some giggles and laughter and somebody's yell.
"Why look," said a voice, "this turtle has found
my helmet to be the best shell in town!

"But my motorcycle helmet just isn't for you,
it's not formal wear, it simply won't do.
I know that it's pretty, a shiny round crown,
but it's protection for me when I ride around town."

Shelly frowned and she muttered, "I've done it again.
I've chosen the wrong shell, oh when will it end?"
She thought as she walked back toward Lillypad Lane,
I must find a new shell to fit on my frame.

So sad was poor Shelly about her defeat
that she was not aware she was crossing a street.
Cars swerved this way and that, almost hitting poor Shelly
who jumped and then ducked and then sucked in her belly.

Shelly had barely avoided one vehicle's tire
when she saw something lovely, a shiny orange spire.
Smooth on the outside and shaped like a cone,
it looked like the shell she could finally own.

And though it looked strange, she didn't think twice.
"This funny-shaped thing is really quite nice."
Shelly couldn't help cracking a satisfied grin
before tucking her head and squeezing right in.

And that's when it came, the shouts and the cries,
as Shelly moved homeward with the big orange surprise.
"That turtle," yelled someone, "is taking our cone!
She's walking away from our No Parking Zone!"

Another worker shouted, "I'll get it for you!"
And the slow-moving turtle he went to pursue.
Before she got far, the man had caught up
and removed from her back the pointy orange cup.

Now Shelly was so sad, her hopes had grown thin.
In only one hour the ball would begin!
She had nothing fancy, nothing silky or fine
to wear to the ball down by the lone pine.

So she walked her way back to Lillypad Lane
and when she reached home, it had started to rain.
The dreary drip-drops mixed with a green turtle tear,
because Shelly was sad—she had lost all her cheer.

But then Shelly saw something gleam in the grass:
it was something familiar, but it sparkled like glass.
It looked like her old shell, but now shiny and clean,
washed by the rain to a deep, emerald green!

Shelly's old shell was plain, that much was true,
but rinsed of its dust, it had a lovely green hue.
She slipped smoothly inside her fresh emerald dome
and said these six words: "It feels good to be home."

As fast as a turtle could possibly run
Shelly hurried to the meadow to join everyone.
What a tremendous display of so many creatures
with outfits that showed off all their fine features.

The gophers wore waistcoats and the frogs all were dressed
in black silk tuxedoes and ruby red vests.
The lizards wore leotards and pleated black skirts,
while the mice came to dance in snazzy starched shirts.
The birds wore tiaras, and even the bats
wore polka dot bow ties and tall black top hats.

The dragonflies looked elegant with wings of pure lace
and every raccoon wore a veil on her face.
But it was Shelly herself who commanded attention;
in her emerald shell she was turtle perfection.

She danced through the night with every guest,
each one commending her magnificent dress.
 When asked where she found her wondrous shell,
she couldn't hold back, she just had to tell:
"This is my old shell that once was so plain,
now polished and cleaned by the fresh falling rain."

As she continued her story, she began to know
the truth about beauty: it is a warm, inner glow.
No matter what you may wear or how you might hide,
you can't cover up what you are deep inside.

And after Shelly left the Dragonfly Ball,
she gradually learned the best thing of all.
It was a simple lesson that Shelly now knew:
sometimes what you search for is right inside of you.